Copyright © 2008 by NordSüd Verlag AG, Zürich, Switzerland.
First published in Switzerland under the title *Herr Hase und Frau Bär*.
English translation copyright © 2008 by North-South Books Inc., New York.
All rights reserved.
No part of this book may be reproduced or utilized in any form or by any means, electronic
or mechanical, including photo-copying, recording, or any information storage and retrieval
system, without permission in writing from the publisher.

First published in the United States, Great Britain, Canada, Australia, and New Zealand in 2008
by North-South Books Inc., an imprint of NordSüd Verlag AG, Zürich, Switzerland.
Distributed in the United States by North-South Books Inc., New York.

Library of Congress Cataloging-in-Publication Data is available.
ISBN: 978-0-7358-2208-5 (trade edition).
10 9 8 7 6 5 4 3 2 1
Printed in Belgium

www.northsouth.com

# Wally and Mae

by Christa Kempter · illustrated by Frauke Weldin

NorthSouth

New York / London

One day Wally found a little house in the woods. No one had lived in it for a long time.

"Since no one else wants it," said Wally, "I'll move in."

But even a little house was too big for one rabbit. So Wally put up a sign:

APARTMENT FOR RENT

The next morning, there was a loud knocking at the door. A large bear looked down at Wally.

"I'm Mae," said the bear. "Nice house. A little small, but I like it. I'll take it."

Wally looked up at the bear. "I was hoping for someone a little smaller. A hamster perhaps, or a turtle."

Mae burst into laughter. "*A hamster*! *A turtle*! Not much company there. You need someone fun." She squeezed through the doorway and headed up the stairs. "Like me."

Wally hurried after her. "No loud parties," he said. "And please keep the place clean—especially the window—I insist on clean windows. . . ."

Every morning, Mae slept late. Then she fixed herself two rolls with honey and a pot of hot chocolate. "Have you finished with the paper yet, Wally?" she shouted downstairs. Then she talked on the phone for a bit. After that, it was time for a nap.

Every morning, Wally sprang out of bed at six o'clock sharp,

ate two carrots while he read the paper,

swept the floors,

washed the dishes,

dusted the furniture,

and watered the geranium.

Then he sat down in his armchair
and admired his tidy home.

Every Friday, Wally baked a carrot cake.

And every Friday, Mae tromped downstairs, toddled into Wally's kitchen, and helped herself.

"You could at least knock," Wally grumbled. "Or try baking a cake yourself."

"You're good at baking," said Mae between bites. "I'm good at eating."

At night Wally paced the floor, worrying. What was he going to do about Mae? She tromped around dropping crumbs everywhere. She was not tidy. Her window was so dirty, no one could see through it.

Wally lost his appetite. He grew thinner.

"You look terrible," Mae told him. "You should relax. Take life easy. Like me."

She plopped two pillows under a tree and stretched out for a snooze.

Then one night there was an awful tromping on the stairs. Wally opened his door and peeped out. Bears, *many* bears, were stomping up the staircase. It wasn't long before loud music was blasting through the house.

This was the last straw! In a fury, Wally hopped right up to Mae's apartment. And what did he see?

Two bears playing accordions, two more bears playing fiddles, one bear blowing a trumpet, and Mae laughing and dancing around the room.

"I'm so glad you came, Wally!" she cried. "Come on, let's dance!" And before Wally could utter a word, Mae picked him up and whirled him around until they were both dizzy.

"These are my brothers," said Mae. The brothers grinned and stuck out their sticky paws. They had been eating honey buns. Wally shook each paw. Then there was more music and dancing and honey buns until Wally couldn't keep his eyes open any longer.

"Poor Wally," said Mae. "It must have been too much for him."
And she picked him up and carried him downstairs to his bed.

"Looks awfully uncomfortable, this bed," she mumbled. So she brought Wally two of her own pillows and tucked them under his head.

Wally had never slept so well—or so late. When he finally sat down to breakfast, he couldn't stop thinking about the party. Funny, he thought. It was messy at Mae's, but it was really cozy. And he liked dancing. Wally got a pencil and some paper and began to write.

Dear Mae,

That was a nice party. Why don't you invite your brothers again? Not too often, though. And maybe they could wash their paws.

Sincerely,

Wally

P.S. May I keep the pillows?

That afternoon, Wally hopped upstairs.

"Can I help you clean up after the party?" he asked.
"It's easier when two are doing it."

"Just don't get carried away," said Mae. "I don't want
things too clean for comfort."

"Let's at least wash the window," said Wally. "You can't
see out anymore."

So Mae washed the inside and Wally washed the
outside. Mae grumbled a little under her breath, but she
worked with Wally until the sun went down.

Then suddenly Mae cried, "Look! I can see the moon out my window!"

And sure enough, there was the moon glowing through the newly cleaned window.

"Wow!" Mae whispered. "There's something to be said for a clean window."

Wally nodded. "How about a honey bun now?" he said. "There's something to be said for honey buns, too!"